Big & SMALL™

...eat Britain by HarperCollins Children's Books in 2009.

13 5 7 9 10 8 6 4 2

ISBN: 978-0-00-731976-3

A CIP catalogue record for this title is available from the British Library.

Based on the television series Big & Small and the original script, 'Something's Missing' by Kathy Waugh. Adapted for this publication by Davey Moore.

© Kindle Entertainment Limited 2009.

Printed and bound in China.

HarperCollins Children's Books

MEET
BIG,

MEET
SMALL

It was a beautiful morning. The sky was blue and the sun was shining. All was quiet and peaceful until...

DRRRIIING!

Big's alarm clock rang out. It was time for him to get out of bed, have a good stretch and face the day.

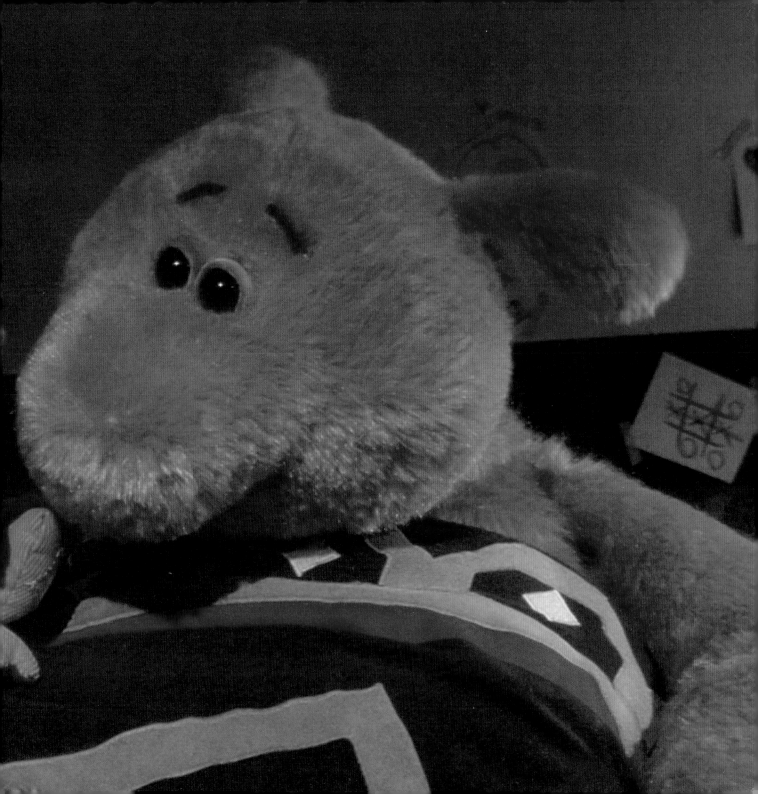

'What a beautiful day,'
said Big. 'Just like every
other day! Except somehow
totally different.'
    Big felt a bit funny – like
there was something
missing. But he couldn't
think what.

Big went downstairs and had a look around.

'One comfy chair. One green fridge. One **tum-te-tum** radio. And one **tra-la-la** piano.'

Everything was exactly where it should be.

TUM-TE-TUM!

TRA-LA-LA!

Big decided to check the garden, to make sure everything was just as he'd left it.

'One shed... some peppers... ten carrots... one wheelbarrow and, let's see, one, two frogs in the lily pond.'

'**Croak**,' croaked the frogs.

'Ah, well,' said Big, 'perhaps nothing's missing after all.'

CROAK!

CROAK!

Back inside the house, Big decided to tidy up. He was busy with the vacuum cleaner when there was a knock at the door. Not just one, firm rat-a-tat but a small and very insistent knock like...

Knock
Knock
Knock
Knock
Knock
Knock

Knock

Knock

Knock

Big looked through the window. But there was nobody there.

Big opened the door. But there was nobody there.

And then a small voice from down below said...

I thought you weren't home!

Big looked down. There was a little orange fellow with a big, brown suitcase.
'Could you get that suitcase for me?' said the orange guy, 'Because I've got **LOADS** more stuff to bring inside.'

'Er... OK then,' said Big, bending down to pick up the case.
'Thanks!' replied the little guy. 'I'll be right back!' And he
zipped away in an orange flash.
He returned almost immediately with more cases and an
inflatable giraffe*.

* Yes, really. An inflatable giraffe!

Pretty soon, there was a big pile of stuff in the middle of the house. It didn't look so tidy any more.

'You're big,' said the little orange chap, looking up at Big.

'And you're small,' said Big.

'I know! I'm Small! And you're Big! Now,' said Small, 'I'll go and hide and if you want me to come for a visit, you can find me! **OK? OK!**'

Small sped off and disappeared. After a second, Small called out from his hiding place.

Big! I'm ready for you to come and find me!

Big went to see if he could find Small.

It wasn't too hard, because Small couldn't stop talking. Not even for a minute.

Small was hiding under a lettuce leaf in the vegetable patch.

Where am I? Where is Small? Let us think. Let us think very hard. 'Let us'? Lettuce! Do you get it? Ha ha! Ah, Big will never find me here!

'Found you!' said Big, bending down and lifting Small out of the lettuces.

'I've never had a visitor before but I think I like it. Will you stay?'

'OK!' replied Small. 'That's settled.' And then he said, 'So! What do you do for big fun around here?'

'We could swing!' suggested Big. 'I love to swing!'

'Great idea!' said Small. Then, after a thoughtful pause, he asked, 'What's a swing?'

Big carried Small over to the apple tree
and set him down on the swing. Small
stood on the seat of the swing. He'd
never swung before. He didn't know how.
'You've got to kick your legs to make it
work properly!' said Big.

Small kicked his legs but nothing much happened.

'Are you sure this is big fun?' asked Small.

'Sit down,' said Big. 'I'm going to push you.'

Small sat down.

Big pulled back the swing and gave it a long, hard push...

WHOOOSSSH!

Small flew off the swing and landed in the flowerbed.
'Ooof!'
'Where are you?' asked Big.
'Over here,' said Small, shaking a leaf from his head.
'Having big fun.'
　　　Big decided that the swing was a bit too big for
　　　Small and so they decided to try something else.

Back inside the house, Big was sitting in his comfy chair looking at a book.

Small sat in his own chair and sighed a big sigh.

'So is this big fun?' said Small. 'Sitting and looking at books and not talking to anybody?'

'Yep!' replied Big. 'I love my books.'

'So far, I'm not having any fun!' said Small. 'I think big fun is different to small fun.'

Big was surprised. He asked what small fun was.

Small climbed up to sit next to his new friend. 'Riding balloons is small fun! And climbing the curtains is small fun. And surfing in the bath! That's small fun! Oh, and skating on ice cubes!' said Small, 'That is so small fun! Woo hoo!'

Big had an idea about what might be fun for Small. He went to get his remote control car - the one with the flashes of lightning down the sides. Small climbed inside the car and picked up the control.

'Number one,' said Big, reading from the instruction booklet. 'Before you drive the car, make sure you read the instructions.'

'Woo hoo!' shouted Small as he drove away in the car.

'Number two,' read Big. 'Always obey the speed limit.'

Small drove the car as fast as it would go. 'Wah-hey!'

'Number three,' Big carried on. 'Always indicate on the turns.'

Small sped round the piano (without indicating). 'Look out!'

'And number four,' said Big, finally. 'Always proceed with caution.'

Small looped right up the wall, across the ceiling and back down the other side. 'Yeee-haah!'

'Now that's what I call small fun!' said Small, squealing to a halt at Big's feet. 'Do you want a ride?'

'**OK**,' said Big, feeling a bit nervous. He stood on the back of the remote control car.

With Big and Small in the car, it couldn't go very far. In fact, it couldn't really go anywhere at all.

But Big and Small laughed. They were having fun together.

Big lifted Small out of the car.
'You know what, Small?' said
Big. 'I thought something was
missing from the house this
morning. And I was right.
YOU were missing!'

'But you found me!' said
Small. 'And I found you, Big!'

Big sighed a happy sigh and
gave his new friend a hug.
They were going to have lots
more fun. Big fun and small fun!

Big & SMALL™

Collect all the books in the series